RATNIP
Dumpster Dive and Dine

BY **CAM HIGGINS** • ILLUSTRATED BY **ALLISON STEINFELD**

LITTLE SIMON
New York Amsterdam/Antwerp London
Toronto Sydney/Melbourne New Delhi

If you purchased this book without a cover, you should be aware that this book is stolen property. It was reported as "unsold and destroyed" to the publisher, and neither the author nor the publisher has received any payment for this "stripped book."

This book is a work of fiction. Any references to historical events, real people, or real places are used fictitiously. Other names, characters, places, and events are products of the author's imagination, and any resemblance to actual events or places or persons, living or dead, is entirely coincidental.

LITTLE SIMON
An imprint of Simon & Schuster Children's Publishing Division
1230 Avenue of the Americas, New York, New York 10020
First Little Simon paperback edition September 2025
© 2025 by Simon & Schuster, LLC
Also available in a Little Simon hardcover edition.
All rights reserved, including the right of reproduction in whole or in part in any form.
LITTLE SIMON is a registered trademark of Simon & Schuster, LLC, and associated colophon is a trademark of Simon & Schuster, LLC.
RATNIP is a trademark of Simon & Schuster, LLC.
For information about special discounts for bulk purchases, please contact Simon & Schuster Special Sales at 1-866-506-1949 or business@simonandschuster.com.
The Simon & Schuster Speakers Bureau can bring authors to your live event. For more information or to book an event, contact the Simon & Schuster Speakers Bureau at 1-866-248-3049 or visit our website at www.simonspeakers.com.
Designed by Brittany Fetcho
Manufactured in the United States of America 0825 LAK
2 4 6 8 10 9 7 6 5 3 1
CIP data for this book is available from the Library of Congress.
ISBN 9781665980975 (hc)
ISBN 9781665980968 (pbk)
ISBN 9781665980982 (ebook)

Contents

CHAPTER 1: Feast for Two — 1

CHAPTER 2: Just a Little Ratnap — 13

CHAPTER 3: A Wild Ride — 25

CHAPTER 4: Landfill Paradise — 37

CHAPTER 5: In the Dumps — 49

CHAPTER 6: Spin the Rat — 59

CHAPTER 7: We Might Be Lost — 71

CHAPTER 8: SOS! — 81

CHAPTER 9: The Home Stretch — 97

CHAPTER 10: Home Sweet Home — 109

CHAPTER 1
FEAST FOR TWO

A full moon, round like a wheel of cheese, shone bright over The City. Streetlights lit up signs on every street corner. And I, Ratnip, was in rat paradise.

Why? you might ask. Well, because I was eating the biggest feast of my life!

Just a few moments ago, I had been walking around The City. I was doing my nightly rounds, looking for something interesting to add to my treasure collection—candy wrappers, string, stuff like that.

Tuffy, my skunk friend, had tagged along too. He isn't a treasure hunter like I am. But ever since I met him in the alleyway behind the ice cream store, he loves joining me on walks around The City.

So far this evening, I hadn't found anything on our walk except a few used tissues. Yuck!

"Let's try the next street," I said. "Maybe we'll have more luck there."

We hadn't gotten very far when Tuffy pointed at something lying on the sidewalk up ahead.

"Look! A bottle cap!" he said.

We circled around the bottle cap, sizing it up.

"Hmmm," I said, stroking my whiskers.

Bottle caps were easy to find in The City. I had to choose carefully which ones to add to my collection, or else my treasure room would be overflowing with them.

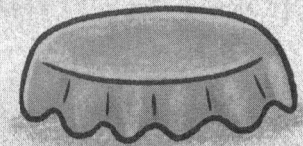

This bottle cap was plain white, and it didn't have interesting patterns on it. So I left it alone.

Just a few steps ahead, we found another bottle cap. This one was yellow with a picture of a lemon printed on it.

"Oh hey! This one is cool!" I said. I showed it to Tuffy before putting it in my bag.

"Whoa," Tuffy said. "What is with all these caps?"

I looked ahead and gasped. All along the sidewalk, bottle caps were strewn everywhere!

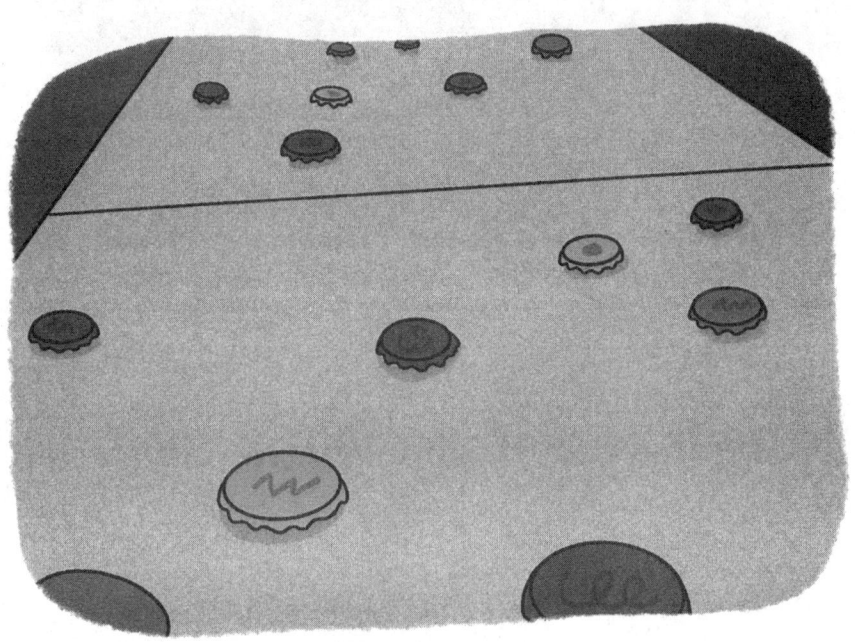

Like I said, bottle caps are common on The City streets. But so many of them, all on the same sidewalk? Something was going on.

Tuffy and I followed the trail of bottle caps down the block, around the corner, and all the way to . . .

the biggest, stinkiest dumpster we had ever seen!

The dumpster was big and green, and it had gigantic wheels. It was standing in the street, resting beside the curb. And—best of all—it was overflowing with trash!

"WOW!" Tuffy and I shouted.

"Forget bottle caps," I said. "That dumpster must be filled with all kinds of treasures!"

"Including treasures that go in our tummy," Tuffy added, rubbing his belly.

We scampered up the wheels on the dumpster. Then we dove right into the sea of trash.

"This is AMAZING!" I squeaked. "It's so amazing, it's almost too good to be true!"

CHAPTER 2

JUST A LITTLE RATNAP

That was how Tuffy and I found ourselves in city critter paradise.

Inside the dumpster, we discovered so much food. I'm talking sandwich crusts, hot dog buns, pickle juice, and apple cores.

The farther we burrowed into the garbage, the more food we found.

There was even a whole container of mac and cheese!

We gobbled everything down. Then we flopped onto our backs and sighed with happiness.

"My tummy feels like it's going to burst," I said.

"Me too," Tuffy agreed. He let out a loud, stinky burp, and we both giggled.

"I should go get Cookie and my siblings," I said. "They would love this dumpster too."

RATNIP FACT: Cookie the raccoon takes good care of my four siblings and me. She can also eat more than the five of us combined!

"Great idea," Tuffy said. "There's enough food here for your whole family—and then some!"

My mind was telling me to get my family. But my body, so heavy with food, was saying it was time for a nap.

"Maybe I'll just take a little break first," I murmured, my eyelids already drooping.

Tuffy responded with a snore.

I didn't know how long we ended up napping. But the next thing I knew, the whole world was shaking and groaning!

"What's happening?" I shouted over all the noise.

"I have no idea!" Tuffy wailed.

Vroom. The dumpster let out a loud growl, and the shaking got a hundred times worse.

Tuffy and I wrapped our paws around each other and held on for dear life. We were tossed this way and that way.

"Ouch!" I cried as I smacked into a plastic carton. Or did the plastic carton smack into me?

Either way, we had to get out of here!

Together, Tuffy and I swam through the trash, trying to make it to the edge of the dumpster. But with everything shaking so much, I could barely tell which way was up.

Finally, Tuffy grabbed the side of the dumpster and popped his head out of the sea of trash.

"Uh-oh," he said.

A second later, I reached his side and poked my head out too. And then I understood.

The dumpster wasn't just shaking back and forth.

No, it was moving forward. Fast!

We were racing through The City on the dumpster's big wheels!

Where were we going? I had no idea. What I DID know was that Tuffy and I were in for a wild ride!

CHAPTER 3
A WILD RIDE

Now that we could see how fast we were going, jumping out of the dumpster was impossible.

"Please, Mr. Dumpster!" I yelled at the top of my lungs. "Please let us out!"

"Dumpsters don't talk," Tuffy pointed out. "I would know. I live inside one."

"Well, guess what?" I replied. "Last I checked, dumpsters didn't go on wild rides, either!"

It sure didn't seem like the dumpster could understand us. At least, it definitely wasn't interested in stopping for us.

All we could do was hold on tight and wait for the dumpster to reach wherever it was going.

Vroom! Vroom!

We squeezed our eyes shut and hugged each other close. I could feel Tuffy shaking, just like I was. We were scared out of our minds!

After what seemed like a lifetime, the shaking finally stopped.

Everything was quiet.

"Do you think it's all over now?" I asked, opening one of my eyes.

Then the whole world turned upside down!

"Oh no! It isn't over!" Tuffy wailed as we sailed through the air.

OOF! Tuffy and I landed on something soft.

And when I opened my eyes, I couldn't believe what I saw.

There were giant mountains of trash to the right. There were even bigger mountains of trash to the left. Heaps upon heaps of garbage, in every direction.

We were in a trash kingdom!

"This place is amazing!" I said.

But Tuffy looked worried.

"Where are we?" he asked. "Are we lost?"

I clucked my tongue and wagged my paw.

"We rats never get lost," I said. "That's a Rat Fact."

That's because I had a method for never getting lost. Just follow the street signs!

But then I realized something.

In this trash kingdom, there were no poles or street signs. There weren't even any streets! Just a bunch of giant piles of trash and a small dirt path running between them.

Tuffy's voice shook as he asked, "What do we do now?"

"Ask a critter," a voice said.

Tuffy and I both jumped as a fly landed on one of the piles of garbage next to us.

"*Bzzz.* If you're lost, ask a critter!" the fly repeated.

I cleared my throat and introduced ourselves.

"I'm Ratnip, and this is my friend Tuffy," I said. "We're not lost, but . . . could you tell us what part of The City we're in?"

"Call me Froo," the fly replied. "And let me be the first to tell you: You are not in The City."

"We're NOT?" Tuffy and I looked at each other, amazed. We weren't in The City AT ALL?

Froo nodded. Then she spread her wings and announced, "Welcome to my home—the landfill!"

CHAPTER 4
LANDFILL PARADISE

Froo led Tuffy and me on a tour of the landfill.

As far as my eyes could see, there was trash, trash, and more trash.

"There's a whole city's worth of trash here," I said.

"You're right. This is all the trash collected from The City," Froo said.

"Trash gets collected from The City?" Tuffy repeated.

Froo snorted. "Well, what did you think? That the trash just magically disappears off the streets week after week?"

Tuffy and I looked at each other and shrugged. That was exactly what we had thought!

It would take a lifetime if I tried to visit every trash can in The City. But now I was seeing it here, all collected in one place. No wonder this landfill was filled with so much stuff!

It's true that Tuffy and I had just eaten the greatest feast of our lives. But here's a **SKUNK AND RAT FACT:** We can always eat more. And more. And more!

We dove into the garbage and chomped away. Froo flew back and forth, flitting from a moldy plum to a moldy peach.

When we finished eating, it was time for treasure hunting. I burrowed through the trash and dug out pencil nibs, straws, even a shiny set of keys.

Now my tummy AND my bag were bulging.

I poked through another pile and felt something sticky and squishy.

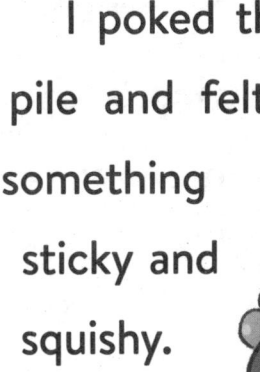

"What's this?" I wondered aloud. I tugged harder, and a long, stretchy string popped out of the pile. It had a gummy paw on the end of it.

I swung the string in the air.

THWAP! That gummy paw was so sticky, it latched onto a plastic fork nearby.

When I pulled the string back, the fork stayed stuck to the paw and came flying right over to me.

"Whoa, this sticky paw is amazing," I said. "I can't wait to add this to my collection when I get home!"

Home.

We were having so much fun, I had nearly forgotten we were so far from home. Looking out at the hills of trash, I realized I had no idea exactly how far we had come. Or how we'd get back.

"How do we get home from here, Froo?" I asked. "Back to The City?"

"There's only one way," Froo said. "Hitching a ride back on the dumpster truck that brought you here."

Tuffy and I saw the dumpster on the other side of the landfill. Its wheels were starting to turn.

"Wait!" Tuffy and I called out.

We began to run after the dumpster, but scampering over the trash was hard work. Garbage is slippery, and slimy, and it slides out from under your paws.

Our little legs were no match for the dumpster's gigantic wheels. The dumpster rumbled down a long path. Soon, all we could see was a cloud of dust and dirt.

As quickly as it had brought us to the landfill, the dumpster had zoomed away. And now we were stranded here . . . so far from home!

CHAPTER 5
IN THE DUMPS

"Oh no!" Tuffy wailed. "We're going to be lost forever!"

"We're not lost, exactly," I said.

I pointed at the dirt path running through the landfill. I could see the dumpster's track marks in the dirt.

"Couldn't we follow this road all the way back to The City?" I asked.

"Maybe," Froo said. "But it would be a really long journey."

Well, that wasn't very encouraging. But I'm a rat who looks on the bright side.

Froo didn't say it was impossible. And if it wasn't impossible, then we had to try.

It was time for

OPERATION GO HOME!

Tuffy and I brushed ourselves off and made our way to the dirt path.

"It was nice to meet you," I said to Froo. "But now Tuffy and I have to go home."

"It's going to be a long journey, so good luck," Froo said. "You might want to bring along a snack."

She handed us some mushy orange slices wrapped inside a paper napkin.

Then Froo flicked her wings and said, "Remember, if you're lost, ask a critter for help."

"Thanks, Froo!" I said. "But we aren't going to get lost."

Tuffy and I set off, following the tracks left by the dumpster wheels.

I picked up a shiny wad of foil to kick as we walked along.

Kick, kick, kick. The foil ball rolled along with us, down the path.

After a while, the piles of trash got smaller and smaller. Then we reached a tall metal fence with a big gate.

"This must be where the landfill ends," I said.

The gate was closed, but that wasn't a problem. We just squeezed through the space between the gate and the dusty ground.

On the other side of the fence, the dumpster's tire tracks continued down the road.

Tuffy whistled while we walked. It was a beautiful night, with barely even a breeze.

I started singing along to Tuffy's whistles.

This is my walking song, we stroll along, all night long. This is my walking song. Oh, won't you sing along?

When the singing made us thirsty, we took turns sucking on the orange slices Froo gave us.

"See, Tuffy?" I said. "We didn't have anything to worry about."

Froo had made the journey sound tough. But so far it had been super easy.

We just had to keep following the dumpster tracks. Then Tuffy and I would be home before we knew it!

CHAPTER 6
SPIN THE RAT

The moon shone down on Tuffy, me, and the dumpster tracks. Every so often, a cloud would float by and the sky would grow dark. But it didn't matter, because rats and skunks can see in the dark just fine.

Up ahead the road forked in two different directions.

I wasn't worried, though. We just had to keep following the tire tracks.

I looked down the road to the left. No tracks that way.

I took a step to the right. There were no tire tracks that way, either!

Tuffy and I crouched low and squinted our eyes. But we couldn't see anything. The dumpster tracks had simply vanished!

"How will we know which way to go?" Tuffy asked.

"Step one, look for a street sign," I reminded my friend.

We looked up. There was not a street sign to be seen.

"In that case . . ." My voice trailed off as I stroked my whiskers.

Then I spied something up ahead on the road to the right. I scampered over to look.

"Tuffy, here's a bottle cap!" I exclaimed. "It must have fallen out of the dumpster! Which means we should take this road to the right."

"Um, Ratnip?" Tuffy said. He pointed to a bottle cap lying on the road to the left, too.

My tail drooped. Well, there went THAT idea.

"Maybe we should ask a critter for help," Tuffy said. "That's what Froo said to do if we got lost."

I watched a line of ants march by.

"I don't feel lost, though," I said. "We just haven't decided which way to go yet."

Plus, I had another trick left in my bag. Whenever I have to make a tough choice, I solve it with what I call . . . Spin the Rat!

I picked up a leaf on the ground and tied it around my eyes.

Rat Fact: If you shut off one of your senses, the other ones get superpowered. Now that I couldn't see anything, my rat nose could focus even more!

"Tuffy, spin me around, please," I said.

Tuffy sent me spinning.

"Whee! I'm getting dizzy!" I said.

By the time I stopped turning, I had no clue which way I was facing.

I raised my snout in the air and sniffed, searching for even the tiniest whiff of home.

Sniff. Sniff. Hmm, was that the scent of human?

I sniffed again. It was faint, but yes, the smell of people was in the air. And people were EVERYWHERE in The City.

"The City is this way," I declared, pointing a paw toward the direction of the smell.

When I untied the leaf, I found myself pointing at the left road.

"Are you sure?" Tuffy asked.

"You can count on my snout, trust me," I answered. "Come on, let's go!"

CHAPTER 7
WE MIGHT BE LOST

Tuffy and I followed the left road as it stretched on. No matter how far we walked, dark buildings loomed around us.

And it was quiet. I didn't hear any cars beeping or neon lights buzzing. There were no machines whirring and no humans stomping around.

I never knew how quiet the world was outside The City.

"Let's make up a new verse for our walking song," I suggested. I took a deep breath and began to sing. *"This is our walking song . . ."*

But Tuffy didn't join in. He came to an abrupt stop in the middle of the road.

"Tuffy," I asked, "what's wrong?"

That's when Tuffy threw himself on the ground and moaned.

"Ratnip, my paws hurt so bad!" he cried. "I can't walk any farther!"

Oh no! I had been so focused on getting home, I hadn't noticed my friend getting tired!

"Let's take a break," I said.

I sat down next to Tuffy and rubbed my own tired paws. I didn't realize how much my paws hurt too.

Without a word, we sucked on the last few orange slices Froo had given us. It already felt like ages since we had been in the landfill with her.

I stared down the road ahead. There were no neon lights or billboards. All I saw were the same dark buildings.

As we sat there in silence, I thought about everything I missed about The City.

I missed my treasure room, of course, and my cozy sock bed.

I missed Cookie. I missed all four of my siblings, Pepperoni and Marg and Veggie and Anchovy.

I missed my cockroach friend, Rochelle. I even missed Ernie the squirrel . . . and he was kind of nutty!

I heard Tuffy let out a little sniffle, and I knew he was missing his home in The City too.

We had been walking forever, but I had no idea how much farther we had to go. Were we halfway? Almost there? Or—*gulp*—even farther from where we started?

I turned to Tuffy.

"I don't want to admit it," I said, "but I think we're lost."

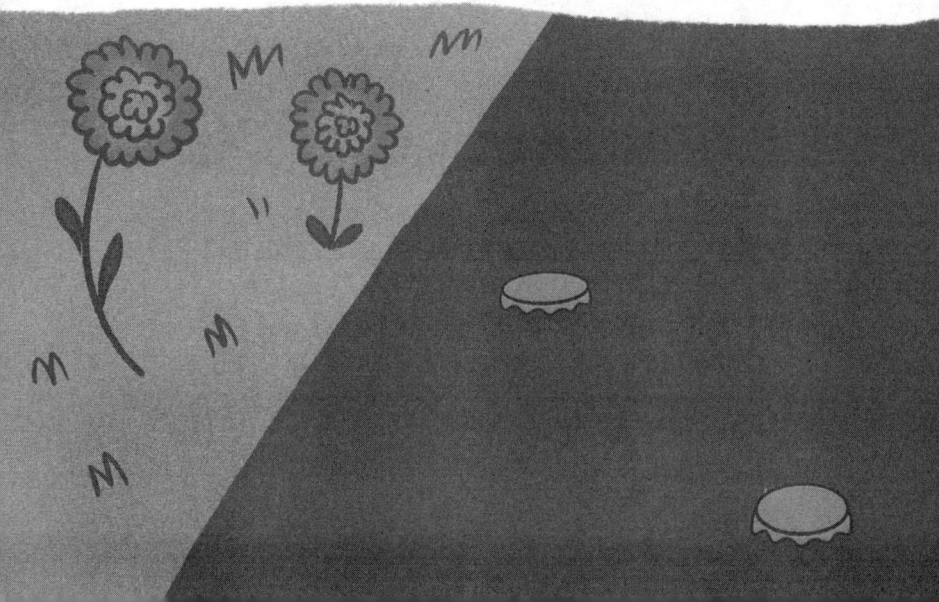

CHAPTER 8
SOS!

Froo said that if we were lost, we should ask a critter for help.

But, like I said already, the street was totally empty. And she didn't tell us what to do if we couldn't find any critters at all.

Just then, the shadow of a bird passed over us.

I jumped and waved my arms, but the bird continued on its way.

"It's no use," Tuffy moaned. "No bird can see us from all the way up there."

"Maybe," I replied. "But they would see an SOS sign."

"S-O-S?" Tuffy asked. "What does that stand for?"

"Um," I said, thinking hard. "Save Our . . . Snouts?"

That didn't sound quite right.

But it didn't matter what it stood for. We just had to spell out the letters SOS on the ground, as big as we could. Then the next critter passing overhead would see the sign and know we needed help.

We got to work right away. I dumped out all the treasures I had stashed in my bag.

This is one of the best things about collecting stuff. My knick-knacks always come in handy when I least expect it!

Tuffy and I carefully arranged bottle caps and leftover orange peels on the ground. We even used the sticky paw rope. Soon we had spelled out three giant letters.

Then we lay down next to our SOS, waiting for a critter to pass overhead. Thankfully, we didn't have to wait long. Soon a dove flew by in the sky.

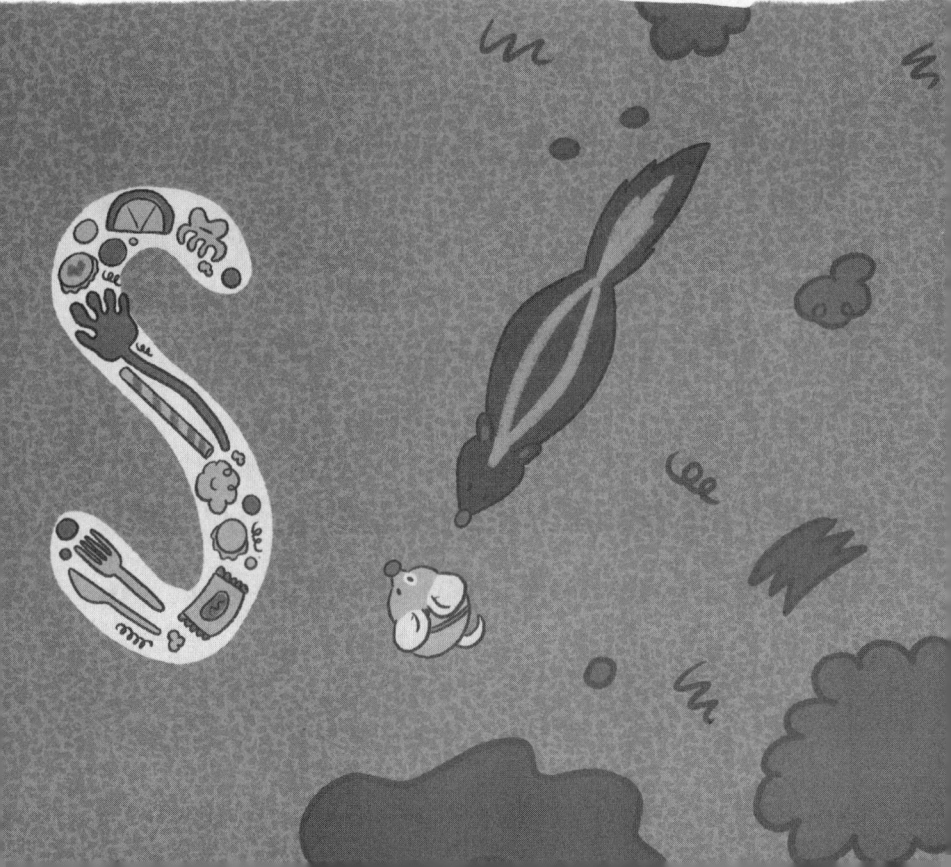

"DOWN HERE!" Tuffy and I screamed.

The dove glided around in a circle before landing right next to us.

"Coo, coo. My name is Dawn," she said. "I've been looking all over for shiny materials to add to my nest, because it isn't big enough for my newborn chicks."

Then she pointed to all the knickknacks that made up our sign.

"You two have collected a lot of bits and bobs there," she said. "Are you building a nest too?"

"I'm Ratnip, and this is Tuffy," I said. "We're not building a nest, but we do need your help."

Tuffy told Dawn how we had gotten lost.

"Can you show us the way to The City?" Tuffy asked.

"We can offer as many of these treasures as you'd like," I said, gesturing to our sign.

I didn't care if she took all the treasures I had collected tonight. That's how desperate I was to go home!

"You're looking for The City?" Dawn clucked. She spread her wings, took off into the sky, and landed on the nearest telephone pole.

"Come on up here, fellas," she said, motioning with her wing.

RAT FACT: We are very good at climbing just about anything. Trees, poles, you name it!

But skunks do not climb as easily as we rats do. So I had to push from below to help Tuffy up.

Finally, we made it to the top of the pole, where Dawn was waiting.

I looked out from our perch and gasped.

A glittering city skyline stretched in front of our eyes. The buildings were standing so tall, they looked like they touched the clouds.

"See? There's The City," Dawn said. "Right in front of you."

Tuffy and I couldn't believe it. If we had just walked a little farther, or climbed a little higher, we would've seen the skyline.

The lights from The City twinkled even brighter than the stars above.

"I didn't know The City was so beautiful," I said.

And I never would have known it if I hadn't gotten lost.

CHAPTER 9
THE HOME STRETCH

Dawn picked up a few pieces of shiny foil from our sign and asked, "May I have these to add to my nest?"

"Of course," I replied. "We can't thank you enough!"

"Thank YOU! This is such a wonderful help," Dawn said before flying off into the sky.

Froo had been right. Asking a critter for help got us un-lost!

I picked up the rest of the treasures and placed them back in my bag. Then Tuffy and I took off, using the city lights as our guide.

It's a funny thing. As soon as I knew we were UN-lost, I felt full of energy again.

Tuffy, who'd had aching paws a few moments ago, was now skipping down the road with delight.

Even so, we were still a long way from The City. With our little paws, I had no idea how long it would take to get home.

The sky was turning from the dark nighttime to a pinkish dawn. Were my siblings wondering why I wasn't home yet? Was Cookie searching for me?

I ran faster. I didn't want my family to worry.

Then, out of nowhere, I heard a loud *vroom*.

Tuffy and I jumped in surprise. When we turned around, we were nearly blinded by two bright lights.

A car was zipping toward us, huffing and puffing. And as it got closer, I saw it wasn't any ordinary car.

It was a DUMPSTER TRUCK!

This dumpster truck looked a little smaller and newer than the one we had ridden in earlier.

But that didn't matter one bit. A dumpster truck was a dumpster truck . . . and it was headed back toward The City!

"Grab on tight, Tuffy," I said. "We are going to catch a ride on that truck!"

Before Tuffy could say anything, I whipped out my sticky paw rope and whirled it like a lasso around my head.

The dumpster truck sped closer and closer.

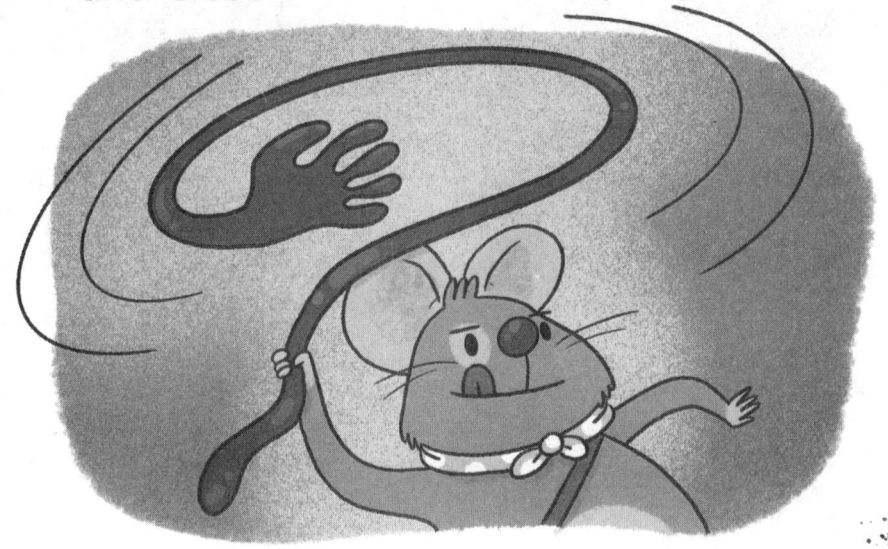

"Ready . . . set . . . NOW!" I yelled, swinging out the rope as far as I could.

THWAP!

The squishy paw stuck onto the side of the dumpster truck. It yanked Tuffy and me up off the ground.

"WHEEEEE!" we yelled, swinging back and forth from the rope as the truck sped forward.

We kept going for a while until the truck paused at a red light. We used that moment to climb up the sticky rope and swing ourselves into the dumpster.

Tuffy and I dropped down into a soft sea of trash.

The light turned green, and the dumpster truck continued its journey.

For the first time since we left the landfill, Tuffy and I sighed in relief.

And you can bet we helped ourselves to another feast of garbage inside the dumpster.

Hey, being lost makes you hungry!

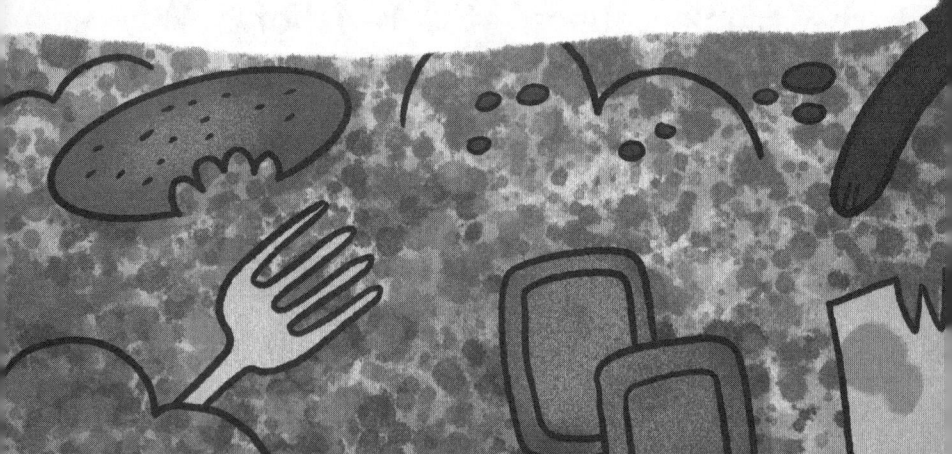

CHAPTER 10
HOME SWEET HOME

Tuffy and I cheered as the truck entered The City. Tuffy even blew kisses to the passing buildings.

"Ah, home sweet home!" I shouted.

Cars beeped at each other. The musty smell of trash filled the air.

Some humans were already awake and walking along the sidewalks.

I let out a big yawn. It was way past bedtime!

At the next stop sign, we both hopped out of the dumpster.

"That was some adventure," I said to Tuffy. "But now I've got to go to bed."

"Me too. Thanks for getting us home, Ratnip," Tuffy said.

We high-fived. Then Tuffy headed toward his dumpster home in the alley, and I set off toward my pizza parlor home.

And there, right in front of the parlor, I ran into Cookie.

"Cookie!" I squeaked, and ran straight toward her for a hug.

"Goodness, Ratnip, where have you been?" Cookie said, scooping me up. "I was just about to go looking for you."

"I might have gotten a teensy bit lost," I told her. "But I found my way home!"

Cookie rubbed between my ears, where she knew I liked it.

"That's my brave little Ratnip," she said.

I leaned in for another hug and squeezed Cookie tight. Finally, I was home.

I tiptoed into the bedroom, trying not to wake my siblings. But they were all lying in their sock beds, awake and ready to pepper me with questions.

"Did you get stuck in a gutter?" said Veggie.

"Did a human find you?" asked Anchovy.

"I bet you climbed to the top of the billboard and couldn't get down!" said Marg.

I laughed and said, "None of those things happened. But I did go to a place called the landfill."

I told them all about the mountains of trash, the treasure, and Froo, of course.

Then I told them about getting lost and seeing the city skyline.

"It was the most beautiful thing I've ever seen," I said.

"Wow," Veggie said, his eyes sparkling. "Will you take us there tomorrow?"

"Tomorrow? I don't think so!" I exclaimed.

I felt like I had been lost enough for a lifetime.

"No, not tomorrow," I repeated with a sleepy grin. "But maybe we'll go the night after that!"

Here's a peek at Ratnip's next adventure!

Everyone knows that rats love garbage. A human's trash is a rat's feast, after all!

But here's a **RAT FACT** you may not know: Not all trash in The City is created equal.

Want sweet treats? Head to a

trash can in the park.

A park will always have cookie crumbs, jam sandwich crusts, and juice boxes. *Yum!*

Looking for a heartier meal? Look no further than the deli trash can. It's got leftover chicken noodle soup containers and greasy corned beef sandwich wrappers.

And if you want a five-star gourmet experience? Oh boy, do I have the perfect trash can for you!

In fact, I was headed there right now.

I scuttled along the streets, past the

park and deli. I zipped over a grate on the sidewalk and got hit with a blast of hot air. Finally, I hit a dead end.

Right there, towering above me, was a big glass building.

It was the brightest building on the block, with huge windows instead of walls. Everything about it was sparkling new. Even the dumpster!

Every fancy building has equally fancy trash, and this building was no different. Inside the dumpster, I found avocado skins, organic snack packs, and oyster shells.